Hidden Pictures

STICKER STORIES

EASTER FUN

illustrated by Anna Pomaska

Grosset & Dunlap
An Imprint of Penguin Group (USA) Inc.

ISBN 978-0-448-42626-6   19 18 17 16 15 14 13 12 11 10

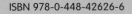

Little Bunny visits Mother Hen to pick up eggs for Easter day.

Can you find **2 eggs**, **5 carrots**, and **4 ducks** hidden in this picture?

Everyone is busy getting ready for the big day.

Can you find **3 lizards** and **6 bugs** hidden in this picture?

The bunnies and their friends
paint the eggs and make pretty baskets.

Can you find **2 butterflies, 4 ducks,** and **6 paintbrushes** hidden in this picture?

Then they hide the eggs
and baskets in the field.

Can you find **4 lizards** and **5 fish** hidden in this picture?

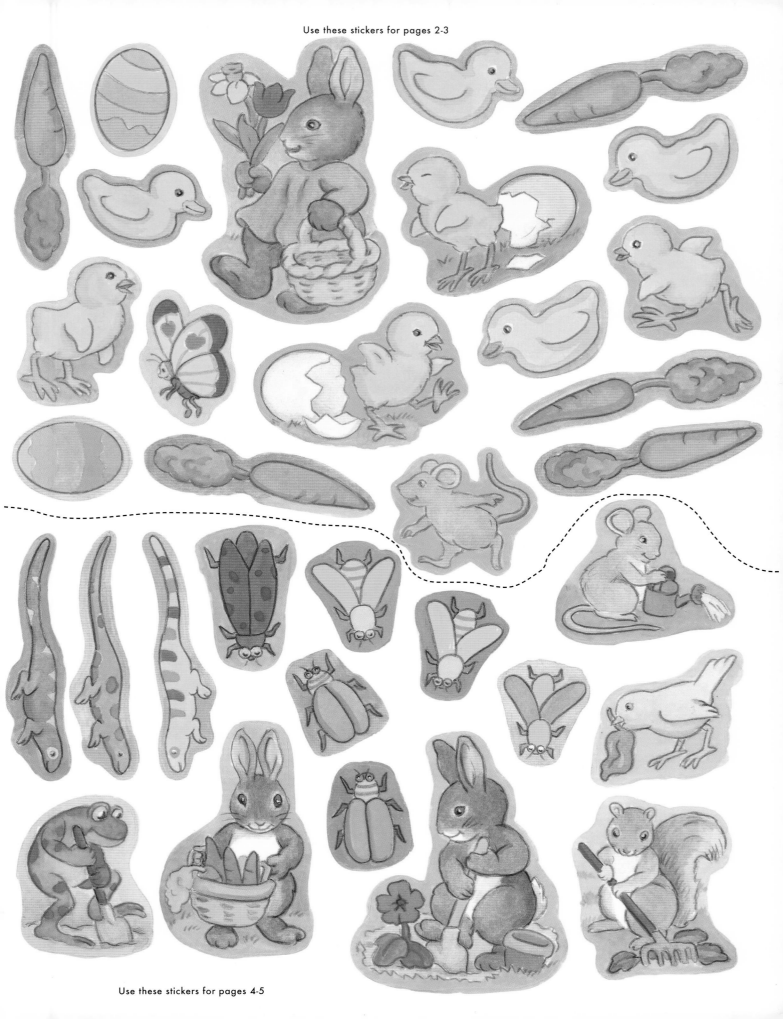

Use these stickers for pages 6-7

Use these stickers for pages 8-9

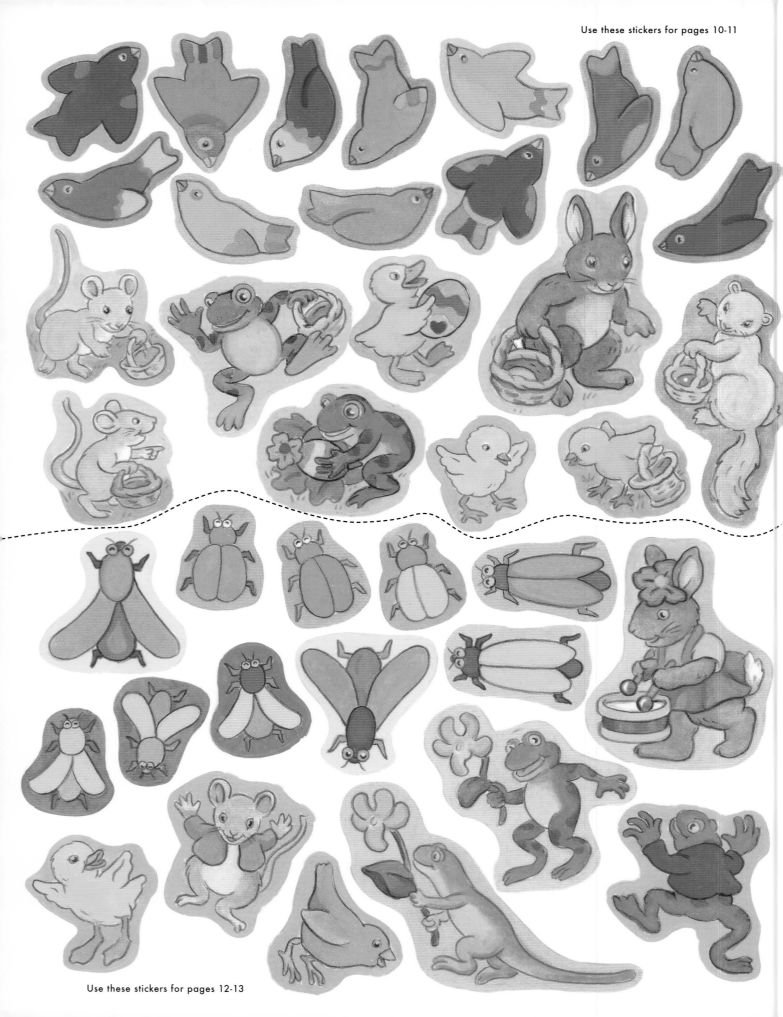

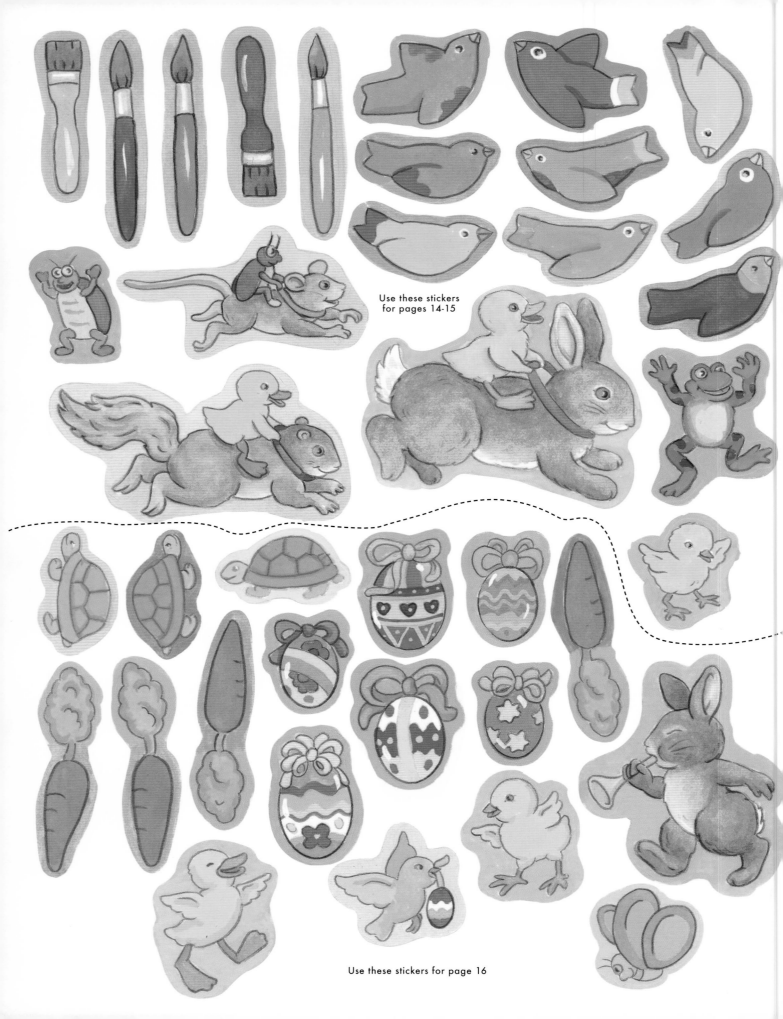

Use these stickers
for pages 14-15

Use these stickers for page 16

Now here comes the fun part—
the Easter egg hunt!

Can you find **12 birds** hidden in this picture?

Look—here comes the Easter parade!

Can you find **10 bugs** hidden in this picture?

It's time for the big race.
Ready, set, go!

Can you find **5 paintbrushes** and **9 birds** hidden in this picture?

Happy Easter!

Can you find 1 butterfly, 3 turtles, and 4 carrots hidden in this picture?